OH, BORIS!

For Dr Elizabeth Marsden – always a smile. – C.W.

For the amazing Early Years Team at Piddle Valley. Thanks for everything! – T.W.

OXFORD
UNIVERSITY PRESS

Great Clarendon Street, Oxford OX2 6DP

Oxford University Press is a department of the University of Oxford.
It furthers the University's objective of excellence in research, scholarship,
and education by publishing worldwide in

Oxford New York

Auckland Cape Town Dar es Salaam Hong Kong Karachi
Kuala Lumpur Madrid Melbourne Mexico City Nairobi
New Delhi Shanghai Taipei Toronto

With offices in
Argentina Austria Brazil Chile Czech Republic France Greece
Guatemala Hungary Italy Japan Poland Portugal Singapore
South Korea Switzerland Thailand Turkey Ukraine Vietnam

Text copyright © Carrie Weston 2007
Illustrations copyright © Tim Warnes 2007
The moral rights of the author and artist have been asserted

Database right Oxford University Press (maker)

First published 2007
This paperback edition first published 2008

British Library Cataloguing in Publication Data available

ISBN: 978-0-19-276337-2 (hardback)
ISBN: 978-0-19-276338-9 (paperback)

10 9 8 7 6 5 4 3 2 1

Printed in China

*With thanks to Michael Bond and HarperCollins for their kind permission
in allowing Paddington Bear to make three and a bit appearances in this book.*

Carrie Weston • Tim Warnes

OH, BORIS!

OXFORD
UNIVERSITY PRESS

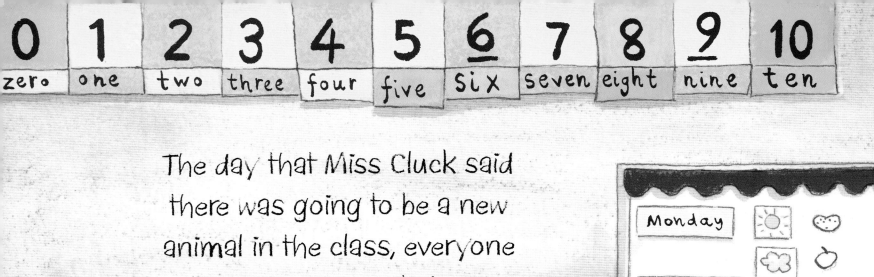

The day that Miss Cluck said there was going to be a new animal in the class, everyone was very excited.

When Miss Cluck said that the new animal was a **bear**, the other animals squealed with delight.

Leticia the rabbit wondered if it might be a fluffy pink bear, like the one on her lunchbox.

Maxwell the mole wanted a floppy brown bear with velvet paws.

The mice hoped for a bear in wellingtons and a duffle coat.

Fergus the fox cub thought any teddy bear would be just fine.

So, when the classroom door opened...

and Miss Cluck introduced Boris...

everyone...

screamed!

For Boris wasn't a teddy bear.

He was an enormous, hairy, scary, grizzly bear!

Miss Cluck found Boris
a seat next to Maxwell.
Boris wanted to
say 'hello' in his
politest voice.

But as he sat
down there
was a loud
crack.

It made Maxwell hide his face in his paws.

'Oh, Boris!'
said Miss Cluck.
'We'd better find you
a bigger chair.'

Miss Cluck gave Boris
a new book and a pencil.
He was very
proud indeed.

With a big, friendly grin Boris turned to show the mice.

But Boris
forgot how
fierce
his teeth
were.

He forgot how
big
his paws
were.

And he forgot how **sharp** his claws were.

 Somehow, the mice got scattered across the classroom.

Somehow, the pages of his new book got ripped.

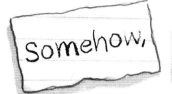 Somehow, there was panic everywhere.

'Boris is too **big**!' cried one little mouse.

'Boris is too **hairy**!' yelled another.

'Boris is too **scary**!' they all squeaked together.

'Oh, Boris!' said Miss Cluck. 'Please try to be more careful.'

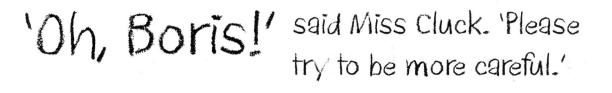

At lunchtime everyone sat together.

There was not enough room on the bench
for Boris, but nobody moved up.

So he sat all by himself
and dipped his big paw
into the large jar of
honey his mummy
had packed
for him.

When lunch was over
Miss Cluck said everyone
could go off and play.

The mice began a game
of hide-and-seek.

Everyone ran
to find a place
to hide.
But Boris
was too
big.

So Boris shut his eyes and counted instead.

'One... two... three...
coming to get you,'
Boris boomed.

'Eeek!'

'Stop!
Stop!'

'No!
No!'

Leticia shook
with fear and
clung to Fergus.

?

Maxwell ran
crying to
Miss Cluck.

'Let's go inside and play
some quiet games,'
said Miss Cluck,
'and Boris, **please** try
to be less scary, dear.'

red

orange

blue

purple

yellow

green

Fergus

Leticia

Maxwell

Marcus
Mouse

Monty
Mouse

Murray
Mouse

The animals sat together in a circle.

There was no space for Boris.

Boris had nobody to play with and nobody to talk to.
Tears filled his big, brown eyes. Large teardrops rolled
down his long nose and splashed to the floor.

'I'm a
scary bear,'
he sniffed.

'I'm a
hairy bear,'
he sobbed.

'I'm just a great
big
grizzly bear.'

It seemed like a very long afternoon.

At last it was time to go home.

Miss Cluck stood and waved as the animals set off through the woods.

Leticia hopped along the bank.

Fergus chased the little mice round a tree.

Maxwell scampered through the leaves.

Boris plodded along far behind.

Suddenly, from a hollow tree leapt....

the
rat
pack!

'Well, well, if it isn't the **boo-babies**,' said the meanest rat.

'Just look at the scaredy-fox and the weedy chicken-licken mice!'

poke!

'Help!'

Leticia, Maxwell, Fergus, and the mice trembled while the rat pack circled round them.

The rats didn't see Boris
plodding along the path.

All Boris could see was lots
of excitement ahead.

He wanted to join the fun.

Huffing and puffing,
Boris stood up tall to greet
the new friends with
his **biggest,** widest
bear grin and. . .

'Quick! Run! It's a hairy, scary, grizzly bear!'

The rotten rats ran away as fast as their skinny legs could carry them.

'But I only wanted to say hello. . .' called Boris.

When Boris turned around,
the other animals cheered.

'Boris is a hairy bear,' they sang.

'Boris is a scary bear,' they chanted.

'We're so glad that
Boris is our grizzly bear!'

Suddenly, Boris felt very shy.
'If you're going to be a bear,'
he said very gently,
'then it's probably best to be a
hairy, scary, grizzly bear.'

The next day at school the animals couldn't wait to tell Miss Cluck how Boris had saved them from the nasty rat pack.

'Oh, Boris!' said Miss Cluck. 'What a good bear you are.'

At story time everyone rushed to gather around Miss Cluck. There wasn't much room once Boris had sat down.

Wednesday

The weather is

Thursday

Friday

But the rest of the class didn't mind one little bit. . .

they all had a soft,
warm place to sit, after all!